# A First-Start® Easy Reader

This easy reader contains only 57 different words, repeated often to help the young reader develop word recognition and interest in reading.

| | | | |
|---|---|---|---|
| a | for | off | sleepover |
| and | fun | on | spooky |
| asleep | good | pajamas | stories |
| bags | have | Papa | tell |
| bedtime | having | party | the |
| Bunny | here | pillow | they |
| cannot | I | popcorn | time |
| cocoa | is | Puppy | to |
| come | it | put | turn |
| comes | Kitty | say | uh-oh |
| end | light | says | was |
| faces | make | show | what |
| falls | makes | silly | |
| fight | Mama | sleep | |
| floor | night | sleeping | |

# Sleepover Party!

by Rita Balducci
illustrated by Susan T. Hall

This new edition published in 2001.

Copyright © 2000 by Troll Communications L.L.C.

Printed in the United States of America.     ISBN 0-8167-6586-3

10  9  8  7  6  5  4  3

Puppy is having a sleepover!

Here comes Kitty!

Here comes Bunny!

It is time for the sleepover party.

Mama makes popcorn.

Papa makes cocoa.

Puppy, Kitty, and Bunny put on a show.

"Bedtime!" says Mama.

They put
sleeping bags
on the floor.

They put on pajamas.

"Bedtime!" says Mama.

"Good night," says Papa.

17

Kitty and Bunny cannot sleep.

Puppy cannot sleep.

19

They make
silly faces.

21

They tell spooky stories.

They have a pillow fight!

Here come Mama and Papa!

Mama and Papa turn off the light.

Kitty falls asleep.
Bunny falls asleep.

Uh-oh! Puppy cannot sleep.

29

"I cannot sleep!"
says Puppy.

30

"Come here," say Mama and Papa.

What a good sleepover—it was fun!
Good night!